THE AMAZING ADVENTURES OF

SCARY

THE SKULL

The Fifth Adventure

Meets the Nasty Romans of Maiden Castle

By

Ron Dawson

Illustrated by Ron Dawson and Sue Burleigh

First Published in 2011 by Mulberry Tree Books

Copyright © Dr Ronald L Dawson 2011

Illustrations Pages 3, 16, 22, 37, 50, 51, 56 & Cover © Ron Dawson and Sue Burleigh 2011

Illustrations Pages 9, 10, 18, 19, 26, 29, 32, 35, 39, 43, 46, 58, 61, 66 © Ron Dawson 2011

Illustration Page 6 © Sue Burleigh 2011

Design and layout by Ron Dawson.

Aerial photo of Maiden Castle by George Allen, 1937

Printed and bound in the UK by Imprintdigital, Exeter EX5 5HY.

This is an old photograph of Maiden Castle Hill Fort taken from an aeroplane in 1937.

MTBooks

Mulberry Tree Books, Mulberry House, Winterborne Stickland, Dorset DT11 0NT
www.mulberrytreebooks.co.uk

ISBN 978-0-9561732-6-3

The Fifth Adventure:
<u>Scary Bones Meets the Nasty Romans of Maiden Castle</u>

Chapter 1

Sasha and Ben were visiting Maiden Castle which is near the town of Dorchester in Dorset. The castle was like no other castle they had ever seen. Instead of being made of big blocks of stone with high walls and tall towers like castles usually are, Maiden Castle is made from lots of long curly whirly grassy hills with deep ditches between them. The castle is very very big and the curly whirly hills seem to go around and around for ever and ever.

The castle stands on top of a high hill and Sasha and Ben were standing at the very top of it. From where they stood, they could see for miles and miles, perhaps even to the very edge of the world itself.

'Isn't it strange, Ben,' Sasha said. 'I've never seen a castle like this ever before in my whole life.'

'That's because it is very very old and not a proper castle. It's really a Hill Fort,' Ben replied. 'It was made thousands and thousands of years ago, perhaps even before the world was made.'

'That's just silly,' said Sasha, 'how could it have been made before the world was made. If the world hadn't been made there wouldn't have been anything to make it from and nowhere to put it when it was made either!'

'Well I don't know about that,' said Ben, 'but I do know that it was made by some people called 'Celts'. Then, after more thousands of years the Romans came along. There was a big fight between the Romans and the Celts right here. The Romans won and captured the Castle.'

Sasha knew a little bit about the Romans. She knew that they lived a long time ago. She also knew that they came from a town called Rome which is in Italy, a country on the other side of the world and perhaps even further away than that, if that is possible. The Romans liked to fight and capture places that didn't belong to them, and they had come to Britain and captured it.

'Anyway,' Ben went on, 'after the Romans captured the castle they built a temple on it, and we are standing right in the middle of all that is left of it now.'

In the grass around them they could see a pattern of two squares made of old bricks and stones. There was a big square and this had a smaller square inside it. These squares of bricks and stone are all that remains of the Roman temple and Sasha and Ben were standing right in the middle of them.

'Oh, we are a Mister Clever Clogs today aren't we?' Sasha said. 'But do you know, Mister Clever Clogs Benjamin, why we are visiting Maiden Castle today?'

Ben didn't know but he didn't want Sasha to know that he didn't know and so he said, 'I bet that you don't know either. You just want me to tell you because you don't know, but I'm not going to tell you. If you are such a Miss Clever Clogs, you can tell me.'

Sasha could see that Ben didn't know and so she said very proudly, 'Well today is the summer solstice!'

'And what, may I ask,' said Ben, 'is a '*summer solstice*?'

Sasha blushed. Ben had caught her out. 'Well I

don't know, I just know that it is!'

'Perhaps Scary Bones might know,' Ben said. 'We could always ask him?'

'Yes, yes,' Sasha called out with delight. 'He probably won't know either, but who cares? I would love to see him again and he will probably like to see us again and to see where we are and what we are doing.'

'So let's call for him to come to see us!' said Ben.

Sasha and Ben had taken the grey box which Scary Bones seemed to live in with them to the castle. Whenever Scary Bones came to see them he would pop out of this box and so they took it wherever they went just in case they ever needed his help.

Ben put the box on the ground and untied the magical piece of **Red String** that held its lid on. The Red String really was magical. Whenever Scary Bones appeared, it would come alive and, when it did, it could think, move, fly, grow, shrink; in fact it could do almost anything at all.

Ben put the Red String by the side of the box and took the lid off. Then he and Sasha began to shout into the box as loudly as they had ever shouted loudly ever before.

'SCARY BONES! CAN YOU HEAR US? PLEASE COME TO SEE US IF YOU CAN!'

The children both stared at the grey box but nothing happened. The grey box just lay there on the ground. It didn't shake, it didn't rattle, in fact it didn't do anything. It just lay there doing what any old grey box would do even if it was being shouted into, and that is nothing at all.

They shouted into it again and again, each time more loudly than the time before.

'SCARY BONES, SCARY BONES! PLEASE, PLEASE COME TO SEE US IF YOU CAN!'

But again nothing happened, nothing what-so-ever. The grey box just lay there, just like it usually did, grey, silent and still. But then they noticed that the Red String had begun to move and wriggle. Then it began to strrrretcccchhhh and strrrretcccchhhh like a sleepy cat that had been cat-napping and had just been woken up. As it stretched and stretched, they heard the faint rattling of bones, skeleton bones. Then a small golden glow appeared in the box and grew bigger and bigger until, quite suddenly and with a loud wwwhhhoooosssshhh, Scary Bones popped out of the golden glow looking as happy and as golden as he had ever looked happy and golden ever before.

The children cheered and cheered and danced with delight around Scary Bones. They cheered and danced so happily around him that Scary Bones began to cheer and dance too. They were all so very very happy to be back together again. Even the Red String began to fly and twirl around them to show that it was very happy too that they were all back together again.

After a short while the children were so out of puff that they couldn't cheer or dance any more. They sat down to recover their puff and the Red String rested itself on their shoulders. Now, as you probably know, because skeletons don't have anywhere to keep puff they don't have any puff at all. And, because they never have any puff, they can never run out of it. So while Sasha and Ben couldn't speak because they were completely out of puff, Scary was very able to speak to them.

'How lovely it is to be with my friends again,' he said and looked around at the Castle. 'And where have you brought me to this time?'

'Phew.....phew,' Ben puffed as he tried to puff in enough puff to speak. 'Phew....phew. This is Maiden Castle, phew.... and right where we are standing, phew.. there was once a Roman temple.'

'And phew...,' said Sasha, who had puffed in nearly enough puff to be able to speak properly now, 'we know that today is the Summer Solstice... phew...phew, but the problem is that we don't know what a Summer Solstice is. Can you tell us what it is Scary Bones?'

The children expected Scary Bones to say, 'Well it's no use asking me, how should I know?' because this was what he nearly always said when he was asked something. But this time he didn't.

This time he stood before them just like a clever clogs teacher and said, 'Well, the summer solstice is the longest long day of sunlight in the whole year. It happens every year on the twenty-first day of June. A long long time ago, the people who lived here worshipped the sun as a sort of God and this was the most important day of the whole year for them.'

The children were so surprised that Scary Bones knew so much about a summer solstice that they asked him, 'How on earth do you know that Scary Bones?'

'Oh, I don't know,' Scary Bones said. 'It's no

good asking me, how should I know? It's just one of those things you know that I know without knowing how I know them you know.' Ben and Sasha were so confused that they laughed out loud. Even the **Red String** began to shake and wriggle as if it were laughing too.

Ben looked at his watch. 'Look, it's nearly twelve o'clock, the very middle of the day, so we are right in the very middle of the very longest day of sunlight in the whole year!'

'So it is,' said Sasha. 'So this is probably the exact time when those people who lived so long ago would have worshipped their Sun God.'

As Sasha said these words the sun seemed to grow in size and brightness. Everything around them began turning to the brightest gold they had ever seen. Everything was so bright and dazzling that they had to shut their eyes as tightly as they could and cover them with their fingers.

As the brightness began to fade they opened their eyes little by little until they were able to peep through their fingers to see what they could see. And, when they did, what they saw was a giant face right in front of them. It was shining as brightly as the sun itself and it had two gleaming eyes which were staring right at them!

It was like no face they had ever seen before. It

was a face made of fire and it was the flames of the fire that made it shine as brightly as the sun. But who did this face belong to? Where had it come from? What did it mean? Why was it staring at them? They didn't have any answers to any of their questions.

Although they didn't know it, they were looking into the eyes and face of the mighty Sun God himself! But although there were lots of things they didn't know about the face, one thing they did know for sure: for them, it was very very scary.

The Face of the Mighty Sun God.

Chapter 2

As the brightness faded away, the children slowly took their fingers away and opened their eyes as wide as they could. They saw that they were standing inside a very strange room. The floors had strange patterns on them and the walls were painted with strange pictures of strange people wearing strange clothes. There was a strange shield hanging very strangely in the centre of the strange room. Perhaps even more strangely, it had the strange giant face it on and it was shining very strangely. Standing before the strange shield with the strange giant face, chanting very strangely, was a strange woman wearing a strange golden crown and strange clothes just like the strange people wearing strange clothes in the strange pictures. It was, as you can tell, all very strange.

The strange woman looked very sad indeed and she was chanting in a strange and squeaky voice with her eyes tightly shut.

'O, mighty Sun God, God of all Celts, giver of all life, king of the heavens and of other places too,' the strange woman chanted. 'Hear my prayer, O mighty Sun God. Send me mighty warriors to drive the nasty Romans away from our lands, away from our holy places, away from Britain for ever and ever and even a little bit longer than that if you can manage it!'

The strange woman stopped chanting and opened her eyes. She seemed to be very surprised to see Sasha, Ben and Scary Bones standing before her and, as soon as she saw them, she closed her eyes and began chanting again.

'O, mighty Sun God, giver of all life and king of the heavens,' she chanted in her strange squeaky voice but sounding more angry than sad now. 'I prayed for mighty warriors and you send me a silly boy and a silly girl and what looks like a silly skeleton. Why, O why, O mighty Sun God?'

'Excuse me,' Ben said to her snootily, 'but I am not a silly boy and my name is Ben!'

'And excuse me,' Sasha said even more snootily, 'I am not a silly girl and my name is Sasha!'

'And excuse me' Scary Bones said as snootily as

any skeleton anywhere has ever spoken snootily. 'My name is Scary Bones and the reason I look like a skeleton is because I am a skeleton and I don't think that I look silly at all! Anyway, who are you to be calling us silly? Silly yourself! And a very strange silly yourself too if I may say so!'

The strange woman stopped chanting and opened her eyes. She looked down at them and she looked angry.

'No, you may not say so!' she said in a voice that wasn't strange and squeaky at all now. Now she sounded and looked like a school teacher who has something very important to say to a school full of naughty children, 'I am Queen Do-you-see-her, Queen of the Celts, great Queen of all Britain and great enemy of the nasty Romans.' She paused and looked at the children and Scary Bones as if she was expecting them to do or say something.

When they didn't do or say anything, she said, 'Now you may bow before me, beg for my forgiveness and then tell me how you came to be here in the temple of the mighty Sun God, and why you are dressed in such strange clothes.'

The children and Scary Bones thought that she must be a mad woman who is so mad that she believes that she is a Queen when she is just a mad woman. But, because they always tried to be very polite to everyone, they bowed before her all the same.

'We beg your forgiveness, O great Queen Do-you-see-her,' they each said to her, trying very hard not to giggle or laugh out loud. 'We don't know how we came to be here and we don't know why you are dressed in such strange clothes.'

'I asked why you were dressed in such strange clothes,' the Queen said a little angrily, 'not why I was dressed in strange clothes! Anyway, none of that matters. What really matters is that I asked the mighty Sun God to send me mighty warriors to drive the nasty Romans from my Queendom and what has he sent me? He seems to have sent me you three! I can only hope that you are three of his greatest warriors cleverly disguised as two silly children in strange clothes and a silly skeleton.'

When she said this, the children were not quite as sure as they had been that she was a mad woman who thought she was a Queen. Perhaps she really was a Queen. And perhaps, just perhaps, they had been whisked back through time by some sort of magic that had gone wrong when she had been praying to her Sun God. But before they had time or chance to say anything, she put her finger to her lips.

'Shush! Be silent now!'

She put her hand next to her ear to listen. 'Shush! I think I can hear the singing of nasty Romans. ..... Yes, I can and they are coming towards us!'

The children and Scary Bones listened very hard. They could hear the sound of men singing, and the sound of their singing was getting louder and louder and closer and closer!

'Two nasty Romans are we,
The nastiest of nasty men,
We march right up to the top of the hill
Then we march right down again,
And when we are there we are there,
And when we are here we are here,
But wherever we march we always seek
The Celt Queen Do-you-see-her.

The men were singing that they were Romans, and that they were very nasty ones too! Scary Bones and the children knew for sure now that they had been whisked back to a time long long ago when there were Romans living in Britain.

'O woe! O woe! Woe is me and all is woe!' the Queen cried. 'It's Maximus and Minimus, the nearly nastiest of all nasty Romans. If they capture us they will throw us all to the starving lions. We must not let them capture us, so quickly, quickly, put on these temple clothes so that they will not see you are three great warriors dressed in strange clothes as a clever disguise!'

As quick as a flash, and perhaps even more quickly than that, she took some strange clothes that were hanging from hooks on the temple wall and gave them to the children and Scary Bones to put on. She gave Sasha and Ben what looked a little like dresses with a belt to tie around the middle. She gave Scary Bones something that looked just like a white sheet off a bed and told him to wrap himself in it.

'But it's a sheet off a bed,' Scary Bones said.

'See, you are silly, just as I thought. It's not a sheet off a bed!' the Queen said. 'It's called a 'Toga' and it's a white one and only very important people are allowed to wear a white toga. Now put it on!'

Because Scary Bones had no idea how to put a toga on the Queen helped him. When he was fully dressed in the toga the Red String wrapped itself around him so that Scary Bones looked very fine and important indeed.

When they were all dressed in the strange clothes, they saw that they looked very much like the strange people who were painted on the temple walls. They realised now that the paintings were pictures of Romans.

The sound of the Romans singing was now much louder. It grew louder and louder and came closer and closer until it came to a stop right outside the door to the temple. After a moment's silence a voice sang out.

'*Come out, come out, whoever you are, two nasty Romans have found you!*'

Inside the temple, the Queen began to wail and groan. 'O woe, O woe, woe is me. All is woe, and all is lost as well as woe. Maximus and Minimus know that we are here in the temple. They won't go away until they have captured us. But wait!' The Queen raised her head towards the sky and smiled. 'In answer to my prayer, the mighty Sun God sent you, my three mighty warriors, and so I have nothing to fear while you are with me.'

Another voice from outside of the temple sang out, *'Come out, come out, whoever you are, or else we'll come in and kill you!'*

'Be quiet now, if I disguise my voice and sing back to them nicely they might go away.' The Queen took a deep breath and sang back to them in her strange squeaky voice, *But who goes there, with voices sweet as the summer air?*

The voices sang back to her, *'You know it to be us, Minimus and Maximus. Now come out here, for we know you to be Queen Do-you-see-her.'*

The children and Scary Bones peeped out from the temple to take a look at the two Romans. They thought that they recognised them but they weren't quite sure. One was tall and thin with a long pointy nose and the other one was short and round with a squashed up nose.

The children decided that the tall thin one must be Maximus. He was holding a long wooden pole which had three steel spikes at the end just like a big dinner fork. The children knew from their history lessons at school that it was called a Trident and that the Romans used them to fight people. In his other hand he held a long shield and on his head he was wearing a silver helmet with silly red hair growing out of it!

The other Roman had to be Minimus. He was short and round and was holding a short sword in one hand and a small round shield in the other. He was wearing a silver helmet with silly red hair growing out of it too, but it looked even sillier than the one Maximus was wearing.

Minimus   and   Maximus

The Queen turned to the children and Scary Bones. 'They know that it is me who is in here. I will have to go out to them. I will tell them to go away and, if they refuse, then you must come to save me, my brave and mighty warriors sent to me by the mighty Sun God himself. You must come save me, if there be a need, from these nearly nastiest of all nasty Romans!'

With that the Queen walked out of the temple to face Maximus and Minimus, the nearly nastiest of all nasty Romans, all on her very own. The children and Scary Bones knew that the two nasty Romans would capture her and then the nasty Romans would capture them too. There was ......
NO ESCAPE!

Chapter 3

The Queen walked out of the temple and stood as proud and as tall as any Queen could ever stand proud and tall in front of two nasty Romans.

'Now nasty Maximus and nasty Minimus, what will you have of me?' she said to them in as Queenly a voice as any Queen has ever spoken in a Queenly voice. 'Tell me now and then be gone with you, for mine eyes cannot bear having to look at you for a moment longer than I must.'

'What we will have of you, your great Majesty,' Maximus said, bowing and laughing, 'is to take you to dine with a King.'

'To dine? To dine with a King no less!' Queen Do-you-see-her cried with delight. 'Ohh..., Good Maximus and Minimus, at last you bend your knee to my royal blood. A King you say?'

'That we do, good Queen,' Minimus said. 'And a right royal king he be too, a king of the jungle! A lion king no less, a lion who feeds on royal blood!'

'And a Roman crowd hungry for the sight of royal blood, for the royal dinner will be held in the great games at the Forum!' In horror, the Queen realised she that was to become a lion's dinner!

Now you should know that although the Romans called them '*games*', their '*games*' were not really games at all. They were really lots and lots of horrible fights between men called Gladiators and sometimes wild animals such as lions. The Romans watched these fights because they didn't have television, computers, bicycles, play stations, skate boards or even tiddlywinks in those days.

The two Romans laughed and laughed and Maximus prodded the Queen with his trident.

'Laugh and prod me while you may,' Queen Do-you-see-her said to them snootily, 'but I will have the last laugh yet!' She turned and boomed out as loudly as she could, *'Come mighty warriors of the mighty Sun God, come to me and save me from these nearly nastiest of nasty Romans!'*

Inside the temple the children and Scary Bones heard her calling to them.

'What shall we do?' asked Ben. 'She believes that we are mighty warriors and that we can save her. What can we do?'

'I have no idea,' Sasha said, 'but we will have to do something to save her.'

'Well I suppose that if we ask them very nicely, the nasty Romans might go away and leave us all alone,' said Scary Bones. 'It's better than not doing anything at all.'

'You're right, Scary Bones,' said Ben. 'It's better than not doing anything at all! So, cross your fingers, toes, knees, eyes and anything else you can cross, and out we go.'

So, after crossing their fingers, toes, knees, eyes and anything else they could cross, they went out of the temple to face the nasty Romans, Maximus and Minimus.

When Queen Do-you-see-her saw the children and Scary Bones come out of the temple, she turned to Maximus and Minimus and boomed again, *'See now, you nearly nastiest of all*

nasty Romans, see how the mighty warriors of the mighty Sun God come to save me. So run, nasty Romans, run! Run for your lives or they will slay you where you stand!'

But, when Maximus and Minimus saw that the mighty warriors sent to the Queen by the mighty Sun God were just two children and a skeleton wearing a toga, they just laughed and laughed as nastily as any Roman had ever laughed nastily.

'Mighty warriors sent to you by the mighty Sun God?' they laughed. 'Well, they are nothing more than two silly children and what looks like a silly skeleton tied up with a piece of silly red string.' And they began to prod and poke the children and Scary Bones with their trident and sword.

'Come on then, come on you three mighty warriors of the mighty Sun God,' they teased. 'We double dare you to save your queen from becoming a lion's dinner, ... and yourselves from a gladiator's blood bath at the Games.'

This frightened the children a lot because they knew that gladiators were men who fought and killed each other with swords, tridents and other nasty sharp things just to entertain hundreds and hundreds of people in great big arenas.

Although Ben was very very frightened he tried to talk to Maximus and Minimus in the nicest way that he could.

'If you wouldn't mind, good sirs, I would ask you first to stop prodding and poking us with your trident and sword. Then I would ask you to go away right now and leave us all alone.'

The two nasty Romans took no notice of Ben whatsoever. They just laughed even more nastily and kept poking and prodding him, Sasha, Scary Bones and the Queen with their trident and sword. They poked and prodded them here, there and everywhere just for the nasty fun of it!

'Please?' Ben said in a voice that trembled like a frightened candle flame on a very and dark windy night. 'Please go away and we won't fight you.'

'Yes,' said Sasha as bravely as she could. 'Please go away. We don't want to fight you but we will if we have to!'

This made the two nasty Romans laugh nastily more loudly than any loud nasty Roman has ever laughed nastily and loudly since the very first loud nasty Roman laughed nastily and loudly.

'And what will you fight us with you silly little people?' Maximus asked. 'Or should I say, you mighty warriors of the mighty Sun God?'

But then, before they even had a chance to answer, Minimus smiled sweetly at them. 'But wait, good Maximus. As they have asked us so very nicely and so very politely, I say that we should go away, go away just as they ask......'

'O thank you, thank you kind sirs,' Ben and Sasha cried with surprise and delight.

But then Minimus went on to say, 'and when we go away, we will take them all with us!'

And both he and Maximus laughed and laughed loudly and nastily again.

'Come now,' Maximus said. 'We have to go to the town of Blandford which has a market place we Romans call a Forum. There we shall sell you to the Roman Governor and Master of the Games. First of all, he will make you fight his nastiest gladiators and then, afterwards, he will feed you to his biggest and hungriest starving lion!'

There was nothing the Queen, children and Scary Bones could do. The two nasty Romans tied them together with a rope which looped around their necks. Then, pulling on the rope, the nasty Romans led them away from the temple and towards the bottom of the castle. At the bottom of the castle there was a road with a pointy signpost which said '*To the Blandford Forum*'.

'Follow the sign!' the nasty Maximus and Minimus shouted at them. 'Today you will be the guests of honour at the great games to be held next to the Blandford Forum.'

With Minimus leading the way, they all began to march towards Blandford town. The Queen, the children and Scary Bones had become the prisoners of two of the nearly nastiest of all nasty Romans. They knew that when they reached the town, they would be made to fight in the nasty Roman Games and that they would all be killed. They knew that for them, there was to be ....

NO ESCAPE!

Chapter 4

The Forum was a market square in the middle of Blandford town and right next to it was a big round building with two great big wooden doors. A sign was hanging from the doors. It said,

> **THE BLANDFORD ROMAN ARENA.**
> **THE GREAT GAMES ARE HERE TODAY.**

It was very quiet in the Forum but, coming from behind the big wooden doors, the Queen, Scary Bones and the children could hear very loud noises. They were the noises of a mighty crowd shouting, cheering, booing and whistling.

Minimus banged on the wooden doors with the handle of his sword. BANG, ... BANG, ...BANG.

'Open the doors, open the doors,' Minimus shouted. 'Let us in. We bring prisoners for the Governor and the games. Let us in.'

An angry voice called out from behind the doors. 'Who dares to bang on the great big doors of the arena when the great games are about to begin?'

Maximus and Minimus called back to the voice behind the great big doors. 'It is us, Maximus and Minimus, loyal nasty Romans of Verymuch Ridiculous, great Roman governor of Britain. We bring him four prisoners for the games.'

'Well that's alright then,' the angry voice behind the great big doors called back. 'As long as you bring prisoners for the games and are not trying to sell anything, then I can let you in.'

The great big doors swung open. Through the doorway the children and Scary Bones could see what looked like a large round playground covered in sand. They realised that it must be the arena and it was here where the games would happen. There were high walls that went all around it and sitting on rows and rows of seats above the walls were thousands and thousands of people shouting, cheering, booing and whistling.

Suddenly the crowd stopped shouting, cheering, booing and whistling. After a moment of silence, a small silly man wearing a bright purple toga and a very silly hat made from leaves entered the arena. As he did, the sound of a thousand trumpets filled the arena. He walked slowly across the arena and climbed some steps which led up to a golden throne. When he reached the throne he stood in front of it and waved to the crowd. As he did, the thousand trumpets fell silent and the crowd began to cheer and shout.

'Hail to Verymuch Ridiculous.

Hail to the great Roman Governor of all Britain.'

'Hail to the nastiest of all nasty Romans, fiddler of

fiddlers and small silly man who wears silly hats.

Hail, hail!'

VERYMUCH RIDICULOUS,
ROMAN GOVERNOR OF BRITAIN,
FIDDLER OF FIDDLERS and
WEARER OF SILLY HATS

The small silly man in the silly hat was Verymuch Ridiculous, the nastiest of all nasty Romans and he was the Governor of all Britain. He waved his hands for the crowds to be silent. When the crowd became silent, Maximus and Minimus dragged the Queen, the children and Scary Bones across the arena to stand right in front of him.

29

'Who stands before me? Speak now or I will have you thrown to my starving lions!' Verymuch Ridiculous asked in a silly squeaky voice.

'Hail, Verymuch Ridiculous, great Governor of Britain, nastiest of all nasty Romans and Wearer of Silly Hats. Our names are Maximus and Minimus. We bring you prisoners for the games and we are selling them very cheaply today.'

Before Verymuch Ridiculous could answer, an angry voice called out. 'You have tricked me, you have tricked me!' It was the same angry voice that had shouted to them from behind the big doors.

'Hear me O great Verymuch Ridiculous, these men tricked me into letting them into the arena. I wouldn't have let them in if I had known that they were going to try to sell you something.'

'But you .....' Maximus started to say something but, before he could say what he was going to say, Verymuch Ridiculous squeaked at him very loudly and very angrily. 'Silence!'

Verymuch Ridiculous was very, very angry because he had been spoken to by Maximus who had not been spoken to by someone who had been spoken to and who would have never had permission to speak or to have spoken to him until they had been spoken to by ..., erm..., well something like that anyway.

'Silence,' Verymuch Ridiculous squeaked very loudly. '*But* nothing ...... The rule is that you are not allowed to speak until you have been spoken to or have been given permission to speak. And you have spoken when you have not been spoken to! And more than that, you have tricked my Keeper of the Great Doors, and the penalty for that is death, death in the arena!'

Maximus and Minimus were too afraid to say anything and, as they couldn't think of anything to say anyway, they didn't say anything.

'They will fight,' Verymuch Ridiculous squeaked to the crowd, 'the baddest and nastiest of my baddest and nastiest gladiators, Biggus Bullyous and Baddus Brutus!'

At once, the sound of a thousand trumpets filled the arena again. Two giant gladiators came into the arena and the crowd cheered and cheered. No-one dared to boo! As the two gladiators marched to the middle of the arena, the crowd shouted, cheered and whistled as loudly as any loud crowd has ever shouted, cheered and whistled loudly.

The Queen whispered to the children and Scary Bones. 'The gladiator with the trident and net is Biggus Bullyous. The one with the short sword and shield is Baddus Brutus. They are both very nasty and so we should get away as quickly as we can!'

Everyone looked towards Verymuch Ridicuous who slowly raised one of his short arms. The crowd stopped cheering, whistling and shouting and the arena became silent. Thinking that this might be a good time to ask to leave, Ben coughed and said quietly, 'Excuse me, sir, erm, great Verymuch Ridiculous, but can we go now?'

'Go? Go? Of course you can't go!' Verymuch Ridicuous squeaked. 'You have just spoken to me without being spoken to and without permission to speak to me or anyone at all. And there's another reason why you can't go. I know who that woman with you is. She is she who calls herself Queen Do-you-see-her, Queen of the Celts and of all Britain! She is my great enemy and so she has to die and, because you are friends of hers and have spoken without being spoken to, you have to die too. Tie them all to the stakes in the arena!'

'Wait, wait!' Queen Do-you-see-her cried. 'A Queen has the right to choose a champion to defend her. If you are, as you say, Verymuch Ridiculous, a proper nasty Roman Governor, you will allow me to choose a champion to fight for my freedom and for the freedom of my friends.'

'O very well,' squeaked Verymuch Ridiculous sounding more than a little irritated, 'but do get on with it! We have all got homes to go to. We can't hang around here all day enjoying ourselves you know!'

Queen Do-you-see-her looked at each of the children and Scary Bones in turn to decide which one she should choose to be her champion. She knew in her heart that not one of them would ever be able to beat Biggus Bullyous or Baddus Brutus in a fight to the death, or even to beat Maximus and Minimus for that matter. But she had to choose one, it was their only hope of escape, and

33

so she chose Scary Bones.

She chose Scary Bones because, with the red string tied around his white toga, he looked the most noble of the three and therefore he was the most suitable to die while defending a Queen.

'I choose....' the Queen said, 'the bony one, the boniest of the mighty Sun God's boniest warriors!'

'So be it,' Verymuch Ridiculous squeaked. 'The bony one is to be Queen Do-you-see-her's champion. To make it a fair fight and, because I don't want anything nasty to happen to my nastiest gladiators, he will fight my nastiest Gladiators without any weapon to defend himself. Now, tie the Queen and the others to the stakes.'

The Queen, Sasha and Ben were taken away and tied to stakes, thick wooden poles, which were stuck into the ground at the end of the arena.

Verymuch Ridiculous raised one of his little arms again and the crowds fell silent. 'Let the great flames for the great Games be lit!'

There were two big bowls full of oil on either side of Verymuch Ridiculous and they were set on fire. As the flames from the bowls leapt into the air, Verymuch Ridiculous squeaked to the crowd in his silliest, loudest and squeakiest voice,

'THE GREAT GAMES' FLAMES ARE LIT!
LET THE GREAT GAMES BEGIN!'

At once, the sound of a thousand trumpets filled the arena and the crowd began shouting, cheering and whistling again. Sasha, Ben and the Queen had each been tied to a stake at one end of the arena. Poor Scary Bones was left to fight Biggus Bullyous and Baddus Brutus all on his own and without anything to defend himself. Maximus and Minimus were still with him but they were clinging onto each other and crying so much that Scary Bones knew they would not be much help to him in the fight to come. He also knew that for him, indeed for all of them, there was .....

NO ESCAPE!

Some Roman soldiers pushed Scary Bones and Maximus and Minimus towards the middle of the arena to get ready to fight Biggus Bullyous and

Baddus Brutus, the biggest, baddest and nastiest of all big, bad and nasty gladiators.

The two gladiators looked to the sky and roared like lions and then marched towards Scary Bones. Maximus and Minimus were so frightened that they stopped crying and ran off to hide behind the children tied to the stakes, leaving Scary Bones to fight the two nasty gladiators all on his own.

But Scary Bones was not frightened one little bit (well perhaps the tiniest of tiny little bits) because he had a cunning plan. It was a very cunning cunning plan that he had used before to save himself and his friends.

First he untied the Red String and threw off the toga he was wearing so that the gladiators and everyone could see that he was in fact a very scary skeleton. Then he turned from white to very bright silver, which is what skeletons do whenever they want to be extra scary and frighten people. Then he began to sway and make the sort of noises skeletons make when they want to frighten people right out of their shoes.

'*OoooOoooo, OOOoooooOO, OOOoooooOOO*'

But this time his cunning plan didn't work! The crowd simply began to laugh and shout. 'He's a silly skeleton, he is just a silly little skeleton!' and they laughed and shouted because they had never seen a skeleton fight with gladiators before.

'Chop him up,' they shouted. 'Chop the skeleton up and then chop them all up and then feed the bones and bits to the starving lions!'

Now that Scary Bones' cunning plan had failed, for him, the children, the Queen, and Maximus and Minimus, there really was ....

NO ESCAPE!

Chapter 5

Biggus Bullyous and Baddus Brutus, the biggest, baddest and nastiest of all Verymuch Ridiculous's big, bad and nasty gladiators were about to fight Scary Bones. Because Minimus and Maximus had run away to hide behind the children, Scary Bones was left to fight the gladiators on his own. But worst of all, Biggus Bullyous had a net and trident to fight with and Baddus Brutus had a sword and shield, while poor Scary Bones had nothing or anyone to help him ......except the Red String!

The Red String would never ever leave Scary Bones to face danger alone and so it flew to Scary Bones' side. Scary Bones knew right away that it had come to help him and that he was no longer alone. Having someone, something, with him to face the dangers before him was all that Scary Bones needed. He changed from being bright silver to being bright purple.

Now, as you may know, when Skeletons are angry or feeling brave they turn purple. And if they are very angry or are feeling very brave, they turn a bright purple. Scary Bones had turned from silver to bright purple which showed that he was very angry and was no longer afraid of either Biggus Bullyous or Baddus Brutus. With the Red String swirling about him, Scary Bones marched towards the two nasty gladiators.

When he got near to them, he stretched out his arm to shake hands with them.

'Greetings good Baddus Brutus and Biggus Bullyous,' he said. 'You know, it really is very silly for us to fight so why don't we shake hands and become friends? That way no-one will get hurt.'

The two gladiators stepped forward as if to do as he asked but then, without any warning, Baddus Brutus swung his sword and chopped off one of Scary Bones' bony arms!

'How's that for a handshake?' Baddus said, 'You look quite armless now!' and both he and Biggus laughed loudly. The crowd cheered and cheered and shouted, 'Chop him up, chop him up!' It looked as if there was NO ESCAPE for Scary

Bones and that he would soon be nothing but a pile of chopped up bones lying in the sand of the arena.

But while the gladiators were busy laughing and the crowd was busy cheering and shouting, Scary Bones picked up his arm bones and clicked them back into place. When the gladiators and the crowd saw what Scary Bones had done and that he was not armless anymore, they became silent.

Never before, in the whole history of gladiator fighting, had anyone ever put back a bit of them that had been chopped off! If someone could put back any of their bits that had been chopped off, it would mean that they could never be beaten!

Baddus Brutus was a little bit afraid now but he was also very angry. Scary Bones had made him look silly in front of all these people and that would not do. 'So, skeleton!' he shouted. 'I am going to chop both of your arms off now, and then we will see if you can put yourself back together again!'

With that Baddus charged towards Scary Bones slashing and waving his sword in the air. Scary Bones did not move at all. Instead, when Baddus was quite near to him, he said quietly to the Red

String which was swirling around his head, 'Now!'

The Red String stopped swirling around Scary Bones' head and flew like an arrow towards Baddus Brutus. Baddus tried to hit it with his sword but he missed and the Red String flew behind him and wrapped itself around his feet and legs. With a loud yell, Baddus tripped and fell flat on his face and dropped his sword and shield.

When Minimus and Maximus saw Scary Bones being so brave, they felt ashamed of themselves. Here was a little bony skeleton who was not afraid of Biggus Bullyous or Baddus Brutus while they had run away and left him to fight the gladiators all alone. Although they thought they could never be as brave as Scary Bones, they didn't want to look like cowards in front of all these people and so, when they saw Baddus fall over, although they were still very afraid, they ran to help Scary Bones.

Before Baddus could get to his feet and pick up his sword and shield, they jumped on top of him and poked him with their sword and trident every time he tried to move. 'Leave him to us,' they called to Scary Bones. 'You fight Biggus Bullyous.'

The Red String untied itself from Baddus's feet and flew back to Scary Bones. Biggus Bullyous had seen what had happened to Baddus and so he swung his big net around him so that the Red String could not tie him up too. Poking his long trident before him, he moved towards Scary Bones and the Red String.

The crowd cheered and cheered. 'Biggus Bullyous will get them now. He will throw his big net over them and they will not be able to escape from it. Then he will poke them to bits with his trident! Hoorah, hoorah for Biggus Bullyous!'

Now that Scary Bones and the Red String knew what Biggus was going to do, they knew what they had to do. They watched as Biggus got closer and closer to them and waited for him to throw his big net. He swung the net around and around his head so that it spread out wider and wider and whooshed in the wind as it went round and round. Then, when he was very close to Scary Bones and the Red String, he threw his net so that it sailed into the air over them like a parachute.

As the net dropped down towards them, Scary Bones flew forward and grasped one corner of it. The Red String flew to another corner and clung onto it. Biggus didn't realise what they were doing and charged towards them but, as he did, Scary

Bones and the Red String flew up into the air and dropped the net over him. They had captured Biggus Bullyous in his own net!

The crowd booed, shouted and whistled. Both of their champions had been beaten and they were angry. They shouted to Verymuch Ridiculous. 'Biggest Bullyous and Baddus Brutus have let themselves be beaten by a silly skeleton. They have shamed the great name of Rome and for that they must die. Make your decision O great Verymuch Ridiculous.'

Now, when a gladiator lost a fight in the arena, the Governor had to decide if he should live or die. If he put his thumb up, the gladiator lived. If he put his thumb down, the gladiator would die.

Verymuch Ridiculous held out his arm and his thumb pointed down. Biggus Bullyous and Baddus Brutus must die!

Like all big bullies who have been defeated or are about to be punished the two nastiest of all nasty gladiators began to cry.

'Please don't kill us good skeleton, we don't want to die, please let us go free.'

Scary Bones looked down at them. 'Before I let you go, will you promise never ever to fight as gladiators again, and that you will go back to your homes and live happily ever after?'

'O yes, yes, cross our hearts and hope to die if we should ever break our promise to you,' they cried.

'Then set them free,' Scary Bones said to Minimus and Maximus.

Maximus and Minmus let Baddus get to his feet and Minimus used his short sword to chop the net away from Biggus so that he could stand up too.

'O thank you, thank you kind skeleton,' Biggus and Baddus said. 'We will keep the promise we made to you. We will leave Britain and return to our homes and families in Rome and we will never ever fight as gladiators again.'

Then, waving goodbye to Scary Bones as they went, Biggus Bullyous and Baddus Brutus, the two nastiest of all nasty gladiators, ran out of the arena like two scaredy custard bunny rabbits.

'Now, quickly,' Scary Bones said, 'we must free Queen Do-you-see-her and my two friends Sasha and Ben and make our escape!'

They ran to where the Queen, Sasha and Ben were tied to the stakes. Minimus chopped through the ropes that held them with his short sword and, in less time than it takes to go from here to there, or even from there to here, the Queen, Sasha and Ben were set free. Now that they were all free they were ready to escape from the arena. But it was not going to be easy.

Verymuch Ridiculous was shaking with anger, in fact he was shaking so much that the leaves started to fall out of his silly hat as if it were a windy autumn day.

'My nastiest of all nasty gladiators have failed me,' he squeaked angrily. 'The time has come to welease mighty Wichard, the hungwy wed lion. Welease Wichard!'

Verymuch Ridiculous was so angry that he couldn't say his 'R's properly.

'Yes, yes,' the crowd laughed. 'Welease Wichard the hungwy wed lion!'

'What do they mean?' asked Scary Bones. 'Welease Wichard, the hungwy wed lion?'

'They mean release Richard, the hungry red lion,' Maximus and Minimus said. 'Richard is the world's most fearsome hungry red lion!'

As they spoke, Scary Bones and his friends heard the loud clang of an iron gate behind them. When they turned to see what had made the gate clang so loudly, they saw, standing right before them, licking its lips and staring right at them, a lion! It was Richard, and Richard was a very big, and a very hungry, and a very fearsome red lion!

Verymuch Ridiculous had released a big hungry red lion to eat Scary Bones and his friends. The crowd roared. 'Richard will eat them all! There's no escape for them now!'

Maximus and Minimus began to shake in their sandals. 'The crowd is right,' they said. 'Richard will eat us all and there really is ...NO ESCAPE!'

Chapter 6

Richard the hungry red lion roared loudly and began to gallop towards Scary Bones and his friends. He was very very hungry and Scary Bones and his friends would make a fine dinner for him. He thought that, as Scary Bones didn't have any meat on him, he might leave him until last and have him as something to chew on later, a little like a dog chews on a bone.

Maximus and Minimus tried to hide behind the Queen and the children, but Scary Bones stepped forward and walked towards Richard. Now normally when Richard galloped towards people, they usually ran away and so, when he saw Scary Bones walking towards him, Richard didn't know what to think or to do, and so he decided to stop.

He put on every brake he had and skidded to a stop just in front of Scary Bones.

'Hello Richard,' Scary Bones said to him. 'Well done. You managed to stop just in time!'

Now, as you may well know, skeletons are able to speak to anything that has a skeleton inside them and, of course, being a lion, Richard had a skeleton inside him. Now again, although you

47

may know this, Richard didn't know it and this was the first time he had ever been spoken to in his own language by someone who wasn't a lion.

'Hello,' Richard replied in surprise and then he asked, 'Where on earth did you learn to speak Lionese?'

'I'll have to tell you about that later,' Scary Bones said. 'There are more important things for us to talk about at the moment. Now tell me, why are you so hungry?'

'Well,' said Richard. 'The nasty Romans keep me locked up in a cage all day and everyday and they don't give me enough food to eat. The only food I get to eat is when they throw people into the arena. I don't like to eat them, but if I don't eat them, then I will starve to death.'

'That's just terrible,' Scary Bones said. 'So if the nasty Romans didn't lock you up in a cage you would be able to go off and find your own food?'

'Yes, that's right,' Richard said, 'but I can't escape. I would have nowhere to go if I did and so, for me, there's no escape.'

'Well, if you help us to escape then you could come with us. If we all help each other, I think we could all escape from the nasty Romans. Will you help us to escape if we take you with us?'

'Oh, yes, yes,' Richard said with delight. 'What do you want me to do?'

'Well,' said Scary Bones. 'This is what we will do. We will all climb onto your back and, when I shout 'Giddy Yap', then you must gallop towards those Romans guarding that open gate. They will be so frightened when they see you galloping towards them that they will run away as fast as their Roman legs can carry them, and then we can will all escape through the open gate.'

'But I'm not long enough to carry all of you,' Richard said. 'I'm only long enough to carry four at a time.'

'That's alright,' Scary Bones replied, 'Maximus and Minimus will just have to run behind us as fast as they can. After all, it was them who got us into this mess in the first place.'

Scary Bones told the others how Richard was going to help them escape and what they were to do. Using the Red String as a rein around Richard's neck, he climbed onto Richard's back and sat there as if he were riding a horse.

'Right,' he called to the others. 'Sasha, Ben and Queen Do-you-see-her, climb up here behind me and hold on tight. Maximus and Minimus, when we make our escape, you will have to run as fast as you can behind Richard.'

Sasha, Ben and Queen Do-you-see-her climbed up behind Scary Bones on Richard's back. Maximus and Minimus stood behind Richard and got ready to run.

'Right,' Scary Bones called again. 'Everyone hold on as tight as you can. Now Richard, on your marks, get set and, *Giddy yap*! *Giddy yap as fast as you have ever giddy yapped!*'

Richard giddy yapped as fast as he had ever giddy yapped straight towards the Roman soldiers guarding the open gate. When they saw Richard giddy yapping so quickly towards them they did just what Scary Bones said they would do. They ran away as fast as their Roman legs would carry them and perhaps even faster than anyone else's legs could have carried them!

With everyone holding on to him as tightly as they could, Richard charged through the gate and giddy yapped along the road which led back to Maiden Castle. And running right behind him, as fast as their Roman legs would carry them, was Maximus and Minimus. They had all escaped!

The crowd in the arena didn't know whether to boo, cheer or laugh. They wanted to boo because their games had been spoiled and there was no one left to fight in the arena. They wanted to cheer Scary Bones and the others because it had been so exciting to watch them escape by riding on the back of Richard the lion. And they wanted to laugh because it had been very funny to see a bony Skeleton and a piece of Red String defeat the nastiest of their nasty gladiators and then ride off on their most fearsome lion as if it were a horse!

As they didn't know quite what to do, they remained silent. The only sound in the whole arena was made by Verymuch Ridiculous who was squeaking as loudly and as angrily as he had ever squeaked loudly and angrily before.

It was the Roman soldiers who had been guarding the gate that Verymuch Ridiculous was squeaking so loudly and angrily at. 'You are all wotten cowards!' he squeaked. 'Wun after them, wun after them. If they escape then you will all be punished weally wottenly, and pewhaps even more weally wottenly than that!' Verymuch Ridiculous was still so angry that he could still not say his 'R's properly.

The Roman soldiers knew that however Verymuch Ridiculous decided to punish them, they would not like it one little bit. So they picked up their weapons and, with their Roman legs running faster than they had ever run fast before, they ran out of the arena after Scary Bones and the others. To escape a really rotten punishment, the

Roman soldiers knew that they had to capture Scary Bones and the others and bring them back to the arena as quickly as they could.

The Roman soldiers soon began to catch them up. Because Richard had not been fed properly and because he was carrying Scary Bones, the Queen and the children, he was running out of puff. Now, just like us, when lions run out of puff they can only run very slowly. Maximus and Minimus were also running out of puff and so they could only run very slowly too. When they looked back towards the arena they could see that the Roman soldiers were running so fast that they would soon catch them up. They were all going to be captured again and this time there would be …….. NO ESCAPE!

Chapter 7

The Roman soldiers were catching up with Scary Bones and the others very quickly.

'It's no good,' Scary Bones said, 'We will not be able to run faster than them. We will have to stop and fight them here and now if we are to stand any chance of escaping.'

Scary Bones climbed off Richard and the Queen, Sasha and Ben followed him.

'Right,' he said. 'This is how we will fight them. Richard will stand in the middle with Maximus and Minimus on his left and with me and the Red String on his right. Queen Do-you-see-her, Sasha and Ben will stand behind us. There are far too many of them for us to escape but at least we will have tried our best, so good luck everybody, good luck and goodbye.'

The Roman soldiers were very close to them now. There seemed to be millions and millions of them, well at least twenty, and they had swords, tridents and shields. There really was ....

NO ESCAPE!

The Roman soldiers came closer and closer to them. Then suddenly, just when the soldiers were nearly close enough to poke Scary Bones and the others with their long tridents, there was a mighty roar. In fact there were two mighty roars! And out of the bushes on either side of them stepped Biggus Bullyous and Baddus Brutus, the two nastiest of nasty gladiators that Scary Bones had set free in the arena!

'O woe! O woe! Woe is me and all is woe!' Queen Do-you-see- her cried, 'it is Biggus Bullyous and Baddus Brutus, we will never be able to defeat them and the Roman soldiers! We are lost and all is woe!'

The two gladiators came marching towards them. Scary Bones and the Red String got ready to fight them again and, although he was very tired, Richard came to stand beside them ready to fight too. When the gladiators were very close to them Biggus Bullyous poked his trident towards Scary Bones.

'Hear me now, bony Skeleton,' he roared. 'You defeated us in the arena but when Verymuch Ridiculous held his thumb down for us to die, you ignored him. You saved our lives and set us free.'

'And now,' roared Baddus Brutus, 'we can repay you for what you did. Now it is our turn to save you and your friends and to let you all escape just as you let us escape!'

With that Biggus Bullyous and Baddus Brutus turned to fight the millions and millions of, well perhaps twenty, Roman soldiers. The Roman soldiers knew that, how ever many of them there were, and there were a lot, they knew that they would never win a fight against Biggus Bullyous, Baddus Brutus and Richard the red lion.

'Hold, good Baddus and good Biggus,' one of the soldiers called out. 'We don't want to fight you, we want to come with you. We want go back to Rome too, we don't want to stay here in Britain, we want to be where our homes and families are, and that's in Rome. Because, as you know and we know, there's no place like Rome.'

When the Roman soldiers were reminded of their homes and families in Rome, all the Romans, including Biggus and Baddus, and Maximus and Minimus, became very homesick and began crying and wailing on each other's shoulders.

'Ohhhhh, whaaaa,' they went. 'Ohhhhh, whrrrrr, whaaaaaaa, whaaaaaaa. We want to go home.'

The sight and sound of so many Romans crying and wailing was just too much for Scary Bones to bear. He stood on Richard's back and shouted to the Romans. 'Then stop crying and go back to Rome. There's no-one who can stop you now, so go back now while you can!'

Biggus Bullyous stopped crying on Baddus Brutus's shoulder for a moment and called up to Scary Bones. 'Yes, we know that but.......' and he began crying again, 'but we don't know the way to go to Rome!'

When Biggus Bullyous said this, the Romans soldiers cried and wailed even more than they had been crying and wailing before.

'Stop, stop,' Scary Bones shouted. 'The way to go to Rome is easy. It's that way!' and he pointed towards the left of the setting sun.

'Is it as easy as that?' Biggus Bullyous asked.

'Well, yes, but perhaps not quite that easy,' said Scary Bones. 'You will also need to ask people you meet on the way which is the right way to go.'

When the Romans heard this they all stopped crying and wailing. 'Three cheers for the bony skeleton,' Baddus Brutus called, 'and then we will leave, all together, for Rome and home!'

The Romans gave three cheers, waved goodbye and set off in the direction that Scary Bones had pointed. As they went they began to sing :

> *'There's no place like Rome,*
> *There's no place like Rome,*
> *Our families all live there,*
> *There's no place like Rome.*
> *There's no place ………'*

Their singing faded away as they disappeared over the top of a nearby hill.

Back in the arena, Verymuch Ridiculous watched helplessly as his soldiers disappeared over the hill. He turned red with anger. The two nastiest of all his nasty gladiators had been beaten by a silly skeleton and a piece of Red String and had run away. The two nasty Romans, who had spoken without having been spoken to, had helped the skeleton to release his great enemy Queen Do-you-see-her and her friends, who had also spoken without being spoken to.

Even his fearsome hungry red lion, Richard, had refused to eat them all and, to make matters even worse, he had helped them to escape from the arena. And now, on top of all of that, all his soldiers had left him to go back home to Rome!

But much much worse for Verymuch Ridiculous was that every one of these things had left him looking very, very silly, even sillier than the silliest of his silly hats. The crowd began to boo because their day at the games had been spoilt and they blamed Verymuch Ridiculous for this. Then they began to laugh at him because he looked so silly standing in front of an empty arena in his silly hat without his nastiest gladiators, his most fearsome hungry lion or any of his soldiers to protect him.

When the crowd laughed at him, Verymuch Ridiculous turned from an angry red to a very bright angry red, and this could mean only one thing; he was about to lose his temper.

Now as you may know, when people lose their temper, they often do the silliest of things, and that's just what Verymuch Ridiculous did. First, he tried squeaking as loudly as he could at the crowd to tell them to stop laughing at him, but this just made him seem even sillier and the crowd laughed even more. Then he tried stamping his feet and crying like a baby, but this just made him seem even more silly than he was already and the crowd laughed louder and louder.

It was then that he had the silliest idea of all the silliest ideas he had ever had. 'This will stop them being nasty to me,' he squeaked to himself. 'This will stop them laughing at me.'

'Wight,' he squeaked angrily at the crowd. 'I will give you something to weally laugh at now!' and then he pushed over the two bowls of burning oil which had been lit at the start of the games.

The burning oil flowed out across the arena and set everything it touched on fire. The fires quickly spread across the Forum and into the town and very soon the whole of Blandford was on fire!

Verymuch Ridiculous was right. The crowd did stop laughing at him. Now, instead of laughing, they were screaming and crying with fear as they tried to escape from the burning arena and town.

Verymuch Ridiculous laughed and laughed. He was absolutely delighted and, whenever he was delighted, he would play his violin, which some people call a fiddle. This is why he was called the 'fiddler of fiddlers' and not because he cheated a lot, as you may have thought. He picked up his fiddle and began to fiddle and dance and, as he fiddled and danced, he sang this song.

> *'Blandford's burning,*
> *Blandford's burning,*
> *In the forum, in the forum,*
> *Fire fire, fire fire,*
> *Pour on water, pour on water.'*

Verymuch Ridiculous was fiddling, dancing and singing as Blandford town burned to the ground!

Chapter 8

When the last of the Romans disappeared over the hill, Queen Do-you-see-her began to dance with delight.

'The mighty Sun God did indeed answer my prayers,' she said. 'When I asked him to send mighty warriors to drive the nasty Romans from my lands, in his great wisdom he sent you, my three heroes. From the very first moment I saw you, I knew that you would be able to do it, and you have!'

Scary Bones was a little puzzled because he remembered that, when Queen Do-you-see-her first saw him and the children, she had called them a silly skeleton and two silly children. But he didn't say anything because he was so very happy that she was so happy. Then he turned to look at Sasha and Ben and was surprised to find that they were looking very, very sad.

'Why are you so sad?' he asked them. 'We have escaped and we are safe now. The nasty Romans have all gone away.'

'Yes,' said Sasha trying to hold back her tears, 'the nasty Romans have gone, gone back to their homes and families, but we will never be able to go back to our home and family.'

'Yes,' said Ben who was holding back his tears just like Sasha, 'we want to go home too.'

Queen Do-you-see-her put her arms around both of the children. 'Dry your tears, my dears. You were sent to me by the mighty Sun God when I asked for mighty warriors. Now I will ask him to take you back to where you came from, and I know that he will do it.'

She pointed towards the distant sky where the temple at the top of Maiden Castle appeared as a dark shadow against a bright red sky. 'But we must hurry,' she said. 'The sun is beginning to set and, when it disappears, this day of the summer solstice will be over. We have to get to the temple before the sun sets. If you don't get back to the temple before this day ends you will have to wait a whole year before the mighty Sun God will be able to take you back to where you came from.'

'Don't worry,' said Scary Bones, 'Richard will take us to the temple in no time at all, and perhaps even faster than that.'

But when they looked at Richard the red lion they saw that he was fast asleep. He was so very tired from all the running and carrying and because he had not eaten for a long time. Scary Bones went to him and whispered softly in his ear.

'Just a little bit further to go, brave Richard,' Scary Bones whispered, 'just a little bit further to the temple at Maiden castle, and there you will have food, all the food you can eat and, afterwards, you will live free for ever and ever.'

Richard slowly opened his eyes. 'I'm sorry, good Skeleton,' he said, 'I was so tired that I fell asleep. But I will do my best to get you all to the Temple before the sun sets.'

Richard struggled to his feet and Queen Do-you-see-her and the children climbed on to his back.

'The Red String and I can fly back,' Scary Bones said, 'so giddy yap, Richard, giddy yap as fast as you can giddy yap to the temple!'

Richard raised himself a little on to his back legs and then set off at the fastest giddy yap he could giddy yap and in no time at all they were back at the temple.

'Quickly,' the Queen cried. 'Quickly, go into the temple. The sun will soon be gone from the sky.'

'No,' said Sasha and Ben together, 'first you must feed Richard. He has been so brave and good that we won't go until he has been fed.'

Queen Do-you-see-her ran into the temple and, in less time than it takes to go from here to there, or even from there to here, came out with all kinds of meat and gave them to Richard to eat.

When Richard had eaten all that he could eat he spoke to Scary Bones. 'Thank you my bony friend, you have saved me from a horrible life in the arena and have set me free. I will go now and I will never fight in the arena again. From now and for ever more, wherever I go, I will only fight for the freedom of people everywhere.'

With that, Richard trotted off towards the setting sun wagging his long tail as happily as he could as he went. When he reached the top of the last hill Richard gave out a mighty roar. Then he rose up on to his back legs as if he was waving 'goodbye' to them all. With the setting sun in the West and the red flames from Blandford town as it burned in the East, the whole sky was the reddest red it has ever been before or since. And against this reddest of all red skies, Richard was the brightest red that he or any other lion has ever been before or since.

Queen Do-you-see-her looked at Richard as he

stood up on his back legs and then, in her queenliest of queenly voices she said. 'From this day forward, the sign of the Red Lion will be the sign of the Kings and Queens of Britain. And when people see the sign of the Red Lion, they will know that it is a sign of bravery and freedom!'

And this is why, wherever you go, you may see a picture of Richard, the Red Lion, on Royal flags, Hotel signs and all sorts of other places and things.

At the top of the hill, Richard turned and walked away. Scary Bones, the children and the Queen watched until the very last bit of the tip of his happy long tail disappeared over the hill into the sunset. Then the Queen, still speaking in her queenliest of queenly voices, said, 'Now good Scary Bones, kneel before me!'

Because she was speaking in such a queenly way Scary Bones did as she asked, although he didn't know why the Queen wanted him to kneel before her. The Queen took a sword from the temple wall and raised it right above Scary Bones' head! What was she going to do? Scary Bones and the children had no idea and Sasha and Ben were about to shout 'Stop!' when the Queen gently lowered the sword and tapped it on each of Scary Bones' bony shoulders.

'Arise, Lord Scary Bones,' the Queen said. 'For your bravery, loyalty and services to your Celt Queen, I make you a grand Celt Lord of Britain.'

Scary Bones was so surprised that, for once, he couldn't say anything at all. The children were so delighted that they clapped their hands and cheered loudly and the Red String did what it always did when it was happy, it swirled and swirled around Lord Scary Bones' head.

Then the Queen spoke in her normal voice again. 'But quickly, the sun has nearly gone from the sky! Into the temple and I will ask the mighty Sun God to take you back to where he found you.'

Scary Bones and the children hurried into the temple and into the strange room where they had first met Queen Do-you-see-her. The strange shield with the strange giant face was still shining very strangely in the centre of the room.

'The mighty Sun God's golden shield still shines, it is still the solstice!' Queen Do-you-see-her cried with delight. 'There is still time. Quickly now, put on your strange clothes and then stand before the shield with your eyes tightly closed!'

Scary Bones, the children and the Red String did as the Queen asked as quickly as they could and she began to chant in her strange squeaky voice.

'O, mighty Sun God, giver of all life and king of the heavens, your mighty warriors have done all I asked of them. Now I beg that you take them back to where they came from, O mighty Sun God, before the Sun sets to bring an end to this longest day of the Solstice.'

Although they had their eyes tightly closed with their fingers held over them, Scary Bones and the children could tell that the strange room had been filled with the bright and dazzling light that had first taken them there. They were also able to tell when the brightness began to fade and, when it did, they opened their eyes little by little until they could peep through their fingers to see what they could see. And, when they did, they saw that they were standing right in the middle of the temple ruins just as they had been at mid-day that very same day.

Perhaps because there was so little time left before the Solstice ended, the mighty Sun God had whisked Lord Scary Bones and the children back so quickly that the Queen did not have time to give Lord Scary Bones an envelope she was holding. When she saw that he and the children were disappearing inside the golden glow, she threw the envelope into the glow after them, but it was too late. Scary Bones and the children had already disappeared when the envelope went into the glow and, when she tried to snatch it back, it had disappeared too.

Scary Bones and the children barely had time to realise that they were back at the top of Maiden Castle again when they heard voices calling loudly from lower down on the hill.

'SASHA! BEN! Where are those children?' It was their parents.

'Time to go again,' said Scary Bones, and he and the Red String jumped into the grey box which was still lying on the grass in the middle of the temple ruins just where they had left it.

'Goodbye my friends, Sasha and Ben,' he said. 'Well, that was another exciting adventure we have had together. Perhaps we will have time to say 'Goodbye' properly next time!'

The children laughed. 'Yes, you always seem to have to leave in a hurry, so perhaps next time. Goodbye Celt Lord Scary Bones, goodbye.' Then, as he always did, Lord Scary Bones disappeared into a golden glow in the grey box. The Red String flew into the box, curled itself up and fell fast asleep in one of the corners. Ben picked up the grey box and he and Sasha began to walk towards where their parents were calling to them.

'Well there you are,' their parents said when they saw them. 'Where on earth have you been? You have been gone for hours and hours. It's almost dark now. Come along now, we need to go home.'

'Yes,' Sasha and Ben said together. 'The sun has almost gone now and with it goes the summer solstice for another whole year.'

They looked towards the sunset which had turned the whole sky bright red. They wondered if their adventure had all been a dream but then, far far away on the very edge of the red sky, they were sure that they could see a lion, a red lion, waving to them. Then, on their way home, they saw all sorts of signs and flags with a red lion on them. They saw Red Lions here, there and everywhere and so they knew that it had not been a dream.

And if you look about you when you go out and about, you too might see Red Lions here, there and everywhere and, when you see them, you may remember this story of how they came to be.

Scary Bones and the children never ever found the envelope that Queen Do-you-see-her threw into the Sun God's golden glow. In fact, do you know, that from that day to this, after the Queen's envelope disappeared into the Sun God's golden glow, it has never ever been seen again?

The End

This is a photograph of the Red Lion Hotel in Wareham, the town where Scary Bones met the Wacky Witches.

The author would like to record his sincere thanks to the pupils and teachers of Anderton Park School, B'Ham; Leehurst Swan School, Salisbury; Fontmell Magna CoE School; and to each and every one of those other children, teachers, parents and friends who contributed in so many ways to the publication of this story.

This is the fifth in 'The Amazing Adventures of Scary Bones the Skeleton' series. The other stories are :

The Lost Dog and Bone : This first adventure tells how Sasha and Ben meet Scary Bones and the Red String for the very first time. The town dogs have all disappeared and Scary Bones has lost a bone. In the adventure that follows they meet the terrible dog-nappers Snatchet and Grabbet, and Mrs. Grumble.

The Pirates of Brownsea Island : Scary Bones, Sasha and Ben are captured by pirates who are after old Captain Grow Bag's treasure which is buried on Brownsea Island. Helped by the island's Red Squirrels, our heroes save it for us all to enjoy for ever.

The Dinosaurs of the Jurassic Coast : Scary Bones, Sasha and Ben are locked in a lost world of monster dinosaurs and cavemen. Helped by Durdle Doorus, the friendliest and happiest of dinosaurs, they escape and the famous Durdle Door is created.

The Wacky Witches of Wareham : The children of Wareham have disappeared and the town is full of sleepy cats. Can Scary Bones rescue Sasha and Ben from the spell of two very strange and unusual lollipop ladies and keep the wizard of Corfe Castle from ruling the world?

Every Scary Bones adventure has a mysterious sealed envelope that should not be opened until the end of the story.

MTBooks

Mulberry Tree Books
Mulberry House
Winterborne Stickland
Dorset DT11 0NT

www.mulberrytreebooks.co.uk